For Louise.

Text copyright © Barbara Mitchelhill 2000
Illustrations copyright © Bridget MacKeith 2000

First published in Great Britain in 2000
by Macdonald Young Books
a division of Hodder Headline Group
338 Euston Road
London
NW1 3BH

The right of Barbara Mitchelhill to be identified as the author
of this Work and the right of Bridget MacKeith to be
identified as the illustrator of this Work has been asserted
by them in accordance with the Copyright, Designs and
Patents Act 1988.

Designed and typeset by McBride Design
Printed in Hong Kong by Wing King Tong

British Library Cataloguing in Publication Data available

ISBN: 0 7500 3003 8

BARBARA MITCHELHILL

Amy's Mermaid

Illustrated by Bridget MacKeith

MACDONALD YOUNG BOOKS

Amy went on holiday with Auntie Sue and her little boy, Joe. They stayed in a cottage by the sea.

There were lots of children on
the beach, so Amy went to play.

First she met a girl.
"I'm Lucy," the girl said. "And this
is my sister."
She was doing a backward roll.

Amy smiled.
"You should see my sister, Pearl," she
said. "She can do handstands."

Soon Amy met a boy.
"I'm William," he said. "And this is my sister."
She was splashing about in the water.

Amy smiled.
"You should see my sister, Pearl," she said. "She can swim like a dolphin."

"Pearl sounds wonderful!" the children said. "Bring her to the beach tomorrow." "OK," said Amy. "I will."

But Amy didn't have a sister.
She had made her up.
"No problem," she said to herself.
"Little Joe can be my sister – if
I change his name."

She showed him how to swim.
She showed him how to do a handstand.
But Joe just wanted to dig in the sand.
When Amy called him 'Pearl' he started
to cry.

"No problem," said Amy to herself. "Auntie Sue can be my sister – if I change her name."

She showed her how to swim.
She showed her how to do
a handstand.

But Auntie Sue wanted to read her
book. When Amy called her 'Pearl',
she got very cross indeed.

Amy walked slowly down the beach.
She wanted to think.

But she saw someone sitting on
a rock. It was a beautiful green
mermaid with long golden hair.

Amy stared at the mermaid and she stared right back. Then the mermaid smiled a wide, friendly smile.

Amy could hardly believe her luck.
A mermaid called Pearl! She was
clever. She could swim. She was *perfect*!
But the mermaid's smile soon faded,

"The tide has gone out," she explained.
"I'm stuck on this rock and I've no one
to play with."
Amy looked around and saw a cart.

"Hop in," said Amy. "We'll go and meet my friends."

She pushed the mermaid along the beach. On the way, they saw an ice-cream van. Pearl wanted to stop.

The man was so busy, he didn't
see Pearl.
"Two choc-ices, please," said Amy.
Pearl loved the ice-cream.

"Come on," said Amy. "We'll
go and meet my friends."
She pushed Pearl along the beach.
On the way, they saw a rock pool.
Pearl wanted to stop again.

She loved the water! She splashed and splashed until her long golden hair was soaking wet.

"Where are you from?" asked Amy
as Pearl's hair dried in the sun.

The mermaid smiled. "My father
is the King of the Blue Ocean.
We live at the bottom of the sea.
We dive for pink pearls.
And we play with sea-horses."

It was nearly tea-time.
"I've got to go," said Amy. "You can
meet my friends tomorrow."
Pearl nodded and smiled. And she
gave Amy a beautiful necklace.

That night Amy dreamed of going
home with Pearl. She dived for pearls
and she played with sea-horses...

The next morning, Amy ran down
to the beach. But Pearl had gone.
On the edge of the water was a
perfect sand-castle. On top there
was a note which read!

The tide came in. Father came to fetch me. P.

Amy felt very sad. Lucy and William
had their sisters. But she had no one.

"Where's Pearl?" asked the children.
"She's gone to see the King of the
Blue Ocean," Amy said.
Nobody believed her.

"*It's true!*" she shouted. She told them
how the king lived in a castle at the
bottom of the sea. And how he dived for
pink pearls and played with sea-horses.

"What a storyteller!" the children said.
"You're wonderful, Amy!"
"No, Pearl is wonderful," said Amy,
looking out to sea. And there, sitting on
a rock, was a beautiful green mermaid
with long golden hair.

Look out for more exciting titles in the Bright Stars series:

Amy's Dragon by Barbara Mitchelhill

When the teacher asks Amy's class to bring in their pets, Amy tells everyone about Oscar. Oscar is amazing! The trouble is Amy has made him up. Then she meets a large, green dragon called Oscar. He's perfect... But can Amy persuade him to go to school with her and be her pet?

Robbie and the Pirate by Margaret Ryan

Robbie's scared of lots of things. He's scared of Growler, the dog. He's scared of Tiger, the cat. And most of all, he's scared of the Grump twins. But he's not scared of Blackbeard, the pirate, who shows him how to stand up to everyone else.

All these Bright Stars can be purchased from your local bookseller. For more information about Bright Stars, write to:
The Sales Department,
Hodder Headline,
338 Euston Road,
London NW1 3BH